exclamation mark

by amy krouse rosenthal & tom lichtenheld

He stood out from the very beginning.

He stood out here.

He stood out there.

It seemed like the only time he didn't stand out

was when he was asleep.

He tried everything to be more like them.

But he just wasn't like everyone else.

Period.

He was confused, flummoxed,

and deflated.

He even thought about running away.

Then, one day . . .

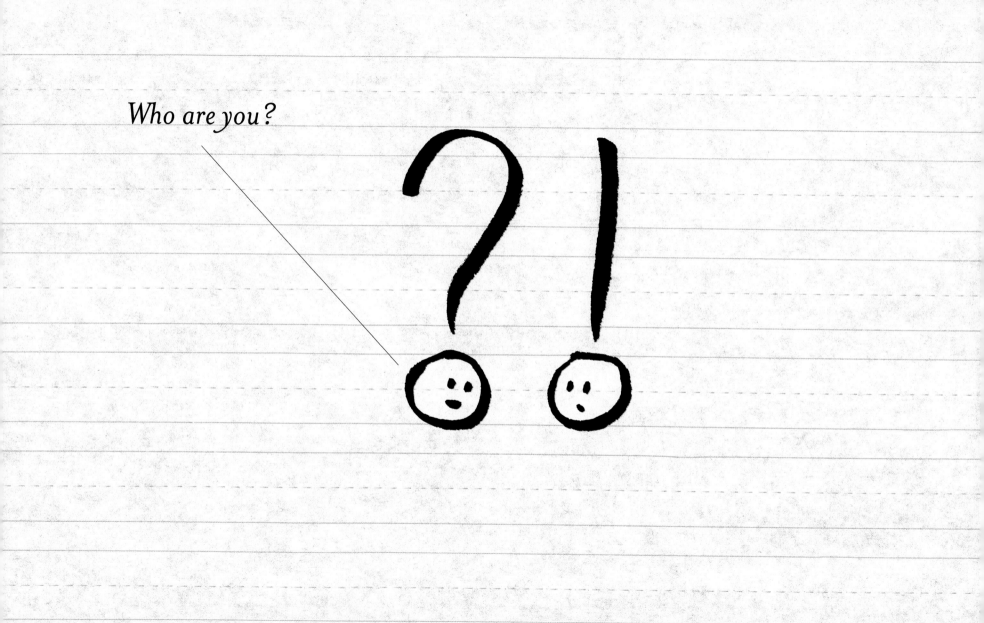

What grade are you in?
What's your favorite color?

Do you like frogs?
What's your favorite ice cream?
When's your birthday?
Know any good jokes?
Do you wanna race to the corner?
Is there an echo in here?
Is there an echo in here?
What's your favorite movie?
Do you know what makes gravity?
Why do you look so surprised?
Am I boring you?
Do you think a snail could go around the world?
So, what do you want to do?
Who's taller, you or me?
What do you want to be when you grow up?

He didn't know he had it in him.

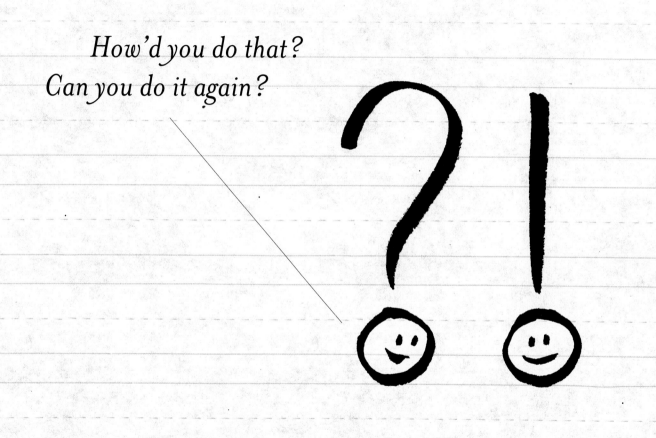

He wasn't sure, so he started small.

That felt right, so he tried something bigger.

And as he pushed himself a bit more,

he discovered a world of endless possibilities.

You're it

Ye

Cool

It was like he broke free
from a life sentence.

Yum

That's great

Thanks

He couldn't wait to show everyone.

Hey guys, it's me

Look what I can do

Of course, there was much exclaiming.

So, with his head held high,

he went off . . .

. . . to make his mark.

ISBN 978-0-545-63130-3

Text © 2013 Amy Krouse Rosenthal   •   Illustrations © 2013 Tom Lichtenheld
All rights reserved. Published by Scholastic Inc.
SCHOLASTIC and associated logos are trademarks and/or registered trademarks of Scholastic Inc.

12 11 10 9 8 7 6 5 4 3 2 1   blastoff!   13 14 15 16 17 18/0
Printed in the U.S.A.   40

First Scholastic paperback printing, September 2013

Typeset in Brandon Grotesque and Mrs. Eaves.
The illustrations were rendered in ink and other exciting materials.
Book design by Tom Lichtenheld and Marijka Kostiw

We dedicate this book to Amy Rennert.

Thank you ☺!

— *Amy and Tom*

That reminds me, did I ever thank you?

Hey, I ask the questions around here, buddy!